Search and SPOT

Animals!

Laura Ljungkvist

Houghton Mifflin Harcourt
Boston   New York

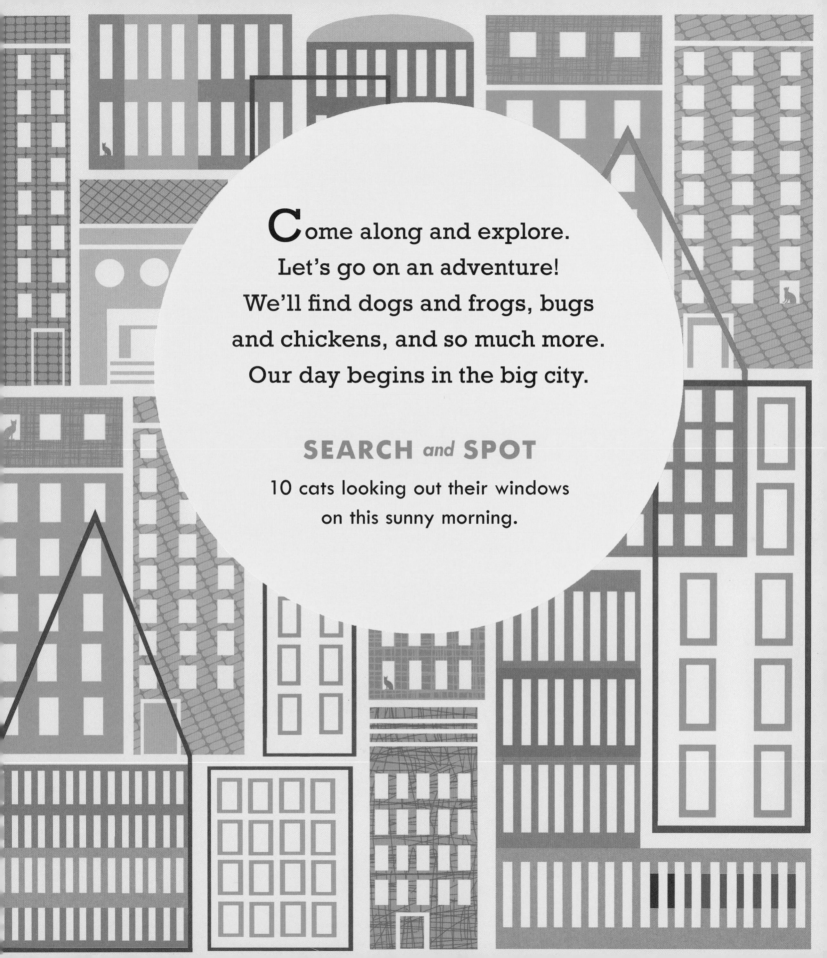

Come along and explore.
Let's go on an adventure!
We'll find dogs and frogs, bugs
and chickens, and so much more.
Our day begins in the big city.

SEARCH *and* **SPOT**

10 cats looking out their windows
on this sunny morning.

Many different kinds
of dogs are out for their
morning walk.
Turn the page, and

SEARCH *and* **SPOT**

all of these furry canines.

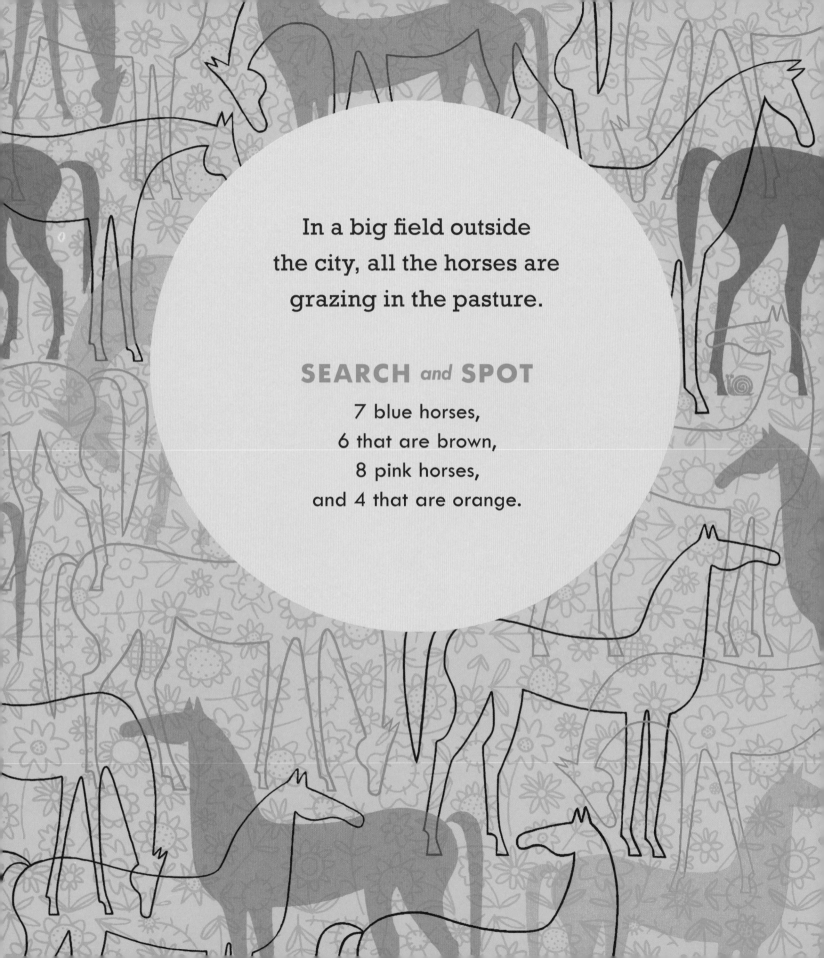

In a big field outside
the city, all the horses are
grazing in the pasture.

SEARCH *and* **SPOT**

7 blue horses,
6 that are brown,
8 pink horses,
and 4 that are orange.

On the farm,
the chickens are running
around the coop after laying
their eggs.

SEARCH *and* **SPOT**

all the chickens you see below.
And can you find a dozen eggs?

Even more cats
live in the country!
Turn the page, and

SEARCH *and* **SPOT**

9 playful kittens,
as well as these
curious cats.

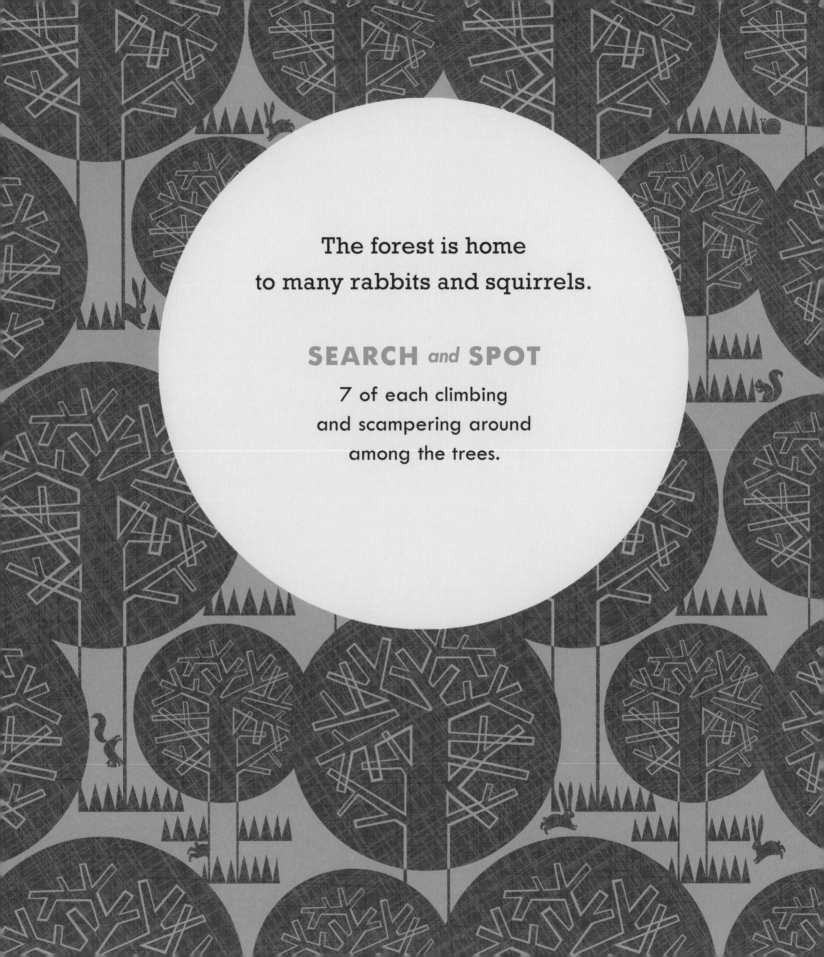

The forest is home
to many rabbits and squirrels.

SEARCH *and* **SPOT**

7 of each climbing
and scampering around
among the trees.

Don't forget the
smallest creatures in the forest.

SEARCH *and* **SPOT**

all the bugs you see below.
And can you spot a daddy longlegs?

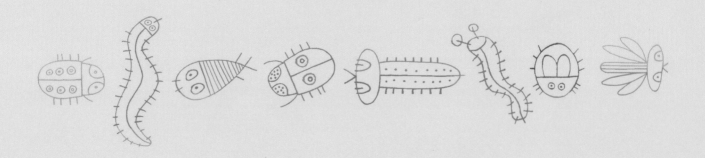

Many big animals roam
the woods. But can you

SEARCH *and* **SPOT**

8 animals that don't belong in this forest?

Here at the lake, see if you can

SEARCH *and* **SPOT**

10 dragonflies

and all the frogs you see below.

Now see if you can

SEARCH *and* **SPOT**

10 tiny blue fish,
7 fish swimming upstream,
and 1 little crab.

In the evening a lot of chirping
can be heard in the forest.

SEARCH *and* **SPOT**

8 black birds,
7 that are quiet,
and 5 tiny baby birds.

Bright moonlight has
awakened the owls.

SEARCH *and* **SPOT**

6 baby owls,
5 hooting owls, and
10 owls that are still sleeping.

Back to the city, where we started our adventure. Can you

SEARCH and SPOT

1 lonely cat out and about
at this late hour?
And last but not least,

this little snail lost his 3 friends
somewhere along the way.
Did you happen to spot them?

Many thanx to Emily van Beek,
Victoria Wells Arms, and John Rudolph
for helping me find my way again.

To Terry Dolphin. To Walter and all
the other guys at Apple Tech Support.

And, as always, to my advisers and
supporters-in-chief, Paul and Violet.

—L.L.

Need help finding any of the animals?

Go to: WWW.HMHBOOKS.COM/SEARCHANDSPOT